To the boys who made
me a wife and a mommy.
And to my grandma that
helped shape me into the
one I've become.
I love you.

Meet Hattie and her friends,
Olive and Amelia.

They are all in first grade together.

They are in Ms. Blooperbluff's class.

Her name always makes them laugh,
so they call her Ms. B for short.

"What do you all want to be when you grow up? I want to be a teacher!" Exclaims Olive.

Amelia says sweetly "I've always wanted to be a doctor. What about you, Hattie?"

Hattie stares at the ground as she says, "I have no idea."

On the school bus ride home, Hattie thinks about what she wants to be when she grows up. She really wants to be a mommy and a wife. "That's not really a job though, is it?" She says to herself.

The little girl walks into her house and is greeted by her mother. "How was school, Hattie?"

"It was good but I'm having a dilemma I don't know what I want to be when I grow up!" Says Hattie worried.

Her mom laughs, "Shouldn't we worry about more pressing matters? Maybe get through supper before deciding on your future."

"No, Mama! Ms. B said we need to decide what we want to be when we grow up THIS weekend."

"Oh, well, what DO you want to be?" Asks Mama.

"I don't really know! What did you want to be when you were a little girl?" wonders Hattie out loud.

Her mama smiles fondly,
"I dreamed of being a chef!"

"Really?" wonders Hattie.

Hattie imagines herself as a world famous chef.

Hattie heads down the hall to see
her brother, Sawyer.

9

"Hey big brother! What do you want to be when you grow up?"

Asks Hattie.

"Well, I want to be a wrestling superstar. But my backup plan is an architect. I'm fairly certain I'm destined to be a wrestler though."

As Hattie leaves her brother's room
she says to herself... "a wrestler?"

11

"No, I don't think I would be a very good wrestler. Besides I'm a lover not a fighter." She remembers her grandparents are over for dinner.

"They'll know for sure!"

13

Hattie walks into the dining room where her Nana and Papaw sit. "Nana, Papaw, what should I be when I grow up?" She eagerly asks.

Nana smiles her sweet smile, "Well, you should do whatever makes you the happiest. Study lots of different things so you become good at everything. Then, there will be no stopping you."
"What she said!" Papaw smirks.

"Hey Mamaw and Papaw, what should I be when I grow up?" Asks Hattie eagerly.

"Well, you can be anything you dream of being!" Smiles Mamaw.

Papaw chimes in "I always thought you would be a pretty cool cowgirl!" Hattie just giggles.

"They always give the best advice. But I still have no idea what I want to be when I grow up. I know, I'll go ask Daddy."

"Hey Daddy! Can I ask you a question?" Wonders Hattie.

"Yes, what can I help you with?" He smiles.

"What did you want to do for a job when you were a kid?"

Daddy thinks for a second, "I wanted to be a farmer."

17

"I'm not sure I want to smell like cow poo all day. Let's go see what Lucy and Waylon think."

"Hey guys, whatcha' doing?" Asks Hattie.

"Oh, you know, just hanging around!" Laughs Waylon,

"Get it?" Lucy sighs... "Yes, Waylon, we get it."

Their bickering always makes Hattie giggle.

"Hey can I ask you all a question?" Hattie chuckles.

"Of course!" Says sweet Lucy.

"What do you want to be when you grow up?"

"Astronauts!" The brother and sister say in unison.

"Hmm." Thinks Hattie.

wow, look at God's amazing creation!
Is this what He sees everyday?"

Hattie was more
confused than ever.

"I know!" She thought,
"I'm going to ask the
wisest person I know."
She heads down the road
to see her grandma.

Her grandma was sitting outside in the shade.
"Hello there Hattie." She said, excited
to see her granddaughter.
"Grandma, I need to ask you a serious question.
What did you dream of being when you were a little girl?"
"I dreamed of becoming a mother and a wife. And that's
exactly what I became." Her grandma smiles.

"No, I meant for
a job." Says a
confused Hattie.

"Don't you know, girl?
That is a job. The most
important job! And now the
fun job is being the grandma!

She giggles.

Hattie plops down under the shade tree.
Thats been it all along! I want to be a mommy and take care of as many babies as I can. My babies, others babies, hurt babies, sick babies, lonely babies, ALL the babies.

I want to be a great mommy
and a wife when I grow up
one day.
And with that Hattie was ready
for school on Monday!

"Well Hattie, have you decided what you're going to be when you grow up?" Her friends ask before class.

"I sure did! I'm going to be a mommy and a wife!"

"That's not a job" Olive laughs.

"Of course it is!" Hattie says proudly. It's the most important job! I'm going to raise all the doctors and astronauts of the world. And I'm going to teach them everything they know!"

The girls laugh and head into the classroom.

So from that day on Hattie always knew her answer when someone asked what she was going to be when she grew up.

And one day she became a loving wife and mother, just like her Grandma.

And God's plan fell into place, as it always seems to do.

About the author

Jess lives with her husband and son in rural Kentucky. She has had a lot of mountains to climb including a lupus diagnosis and kidney dialysis for going on 7 years. But through everything God has seen her through. She wants to spread her love of God and reading to all the little ones.

"All your children will be taught by the Lord, and great will be their peace."
Isiah 54:13

Wishing you bright moments
and special joys
to fill your birthday
and the coming year
with warmth and happiness.

Happy Birthday
Love
Grandpa & Grandma

Made in the USA
Monee, IL
23 August 2021